by Mavis Jukes

I'll See You in My Dreams

illustrated by Stacey Schuett

ALFRED A. KNOPF NEW YORK

Mavis Jukes and Stacey Schuett have joined together to make this
book a farewell tribute to the author's brother.

THIS IS A BORZOI BOOK PUBLISHED BY ALFRED A. KNOPF, INC.

Text copyright © 1993 by Mavis Jukes
Illustrations copyright © 1993 by Stacey Schuett

Library of Congress Cataloging-in-Publication Data

Jukes, Mavis.   I'll see you in my dreams / by Mavis Jukes;
illustrated by Stacey Schuett.   p.   cm.
Summary: A girl preparing to visit her seriously ill uncle in the
hospital imagines being a skywriter and flying over his bed with a
message of love.
ISBN 0-679-82690-4 (trade) — ISBN 0-679-92690-9 (lib. bdg.)
[1. Skywriting—Fiction.   2. Airplanes—Fiction.
3. Uncles—Fiction.   4. Terminally ill—Fiction.]
I. Schuett, Stacey, ill.   II. Title.
PZ7.J9294I1   1993   [E]—dc20   91-47605

Manufactured in the United States of America
2   4   6   8   0   9   7   5   3   1

For Ken

If she were a skywriter, she would wait for the sky to turn pink and blue — the colors of dusk or dawn. There would be only one star out: Venus.

She would put on a brown leather Amelia Earhart jacket and a silk scarf. There would be an abandoned airstrip in the woods, past a cranberry bog. Mist would be rising from the bog as she walked to the airstrip, alone.

Her plane would be a biplane—an old one, made of fabric
and wood. It would be sitting in the grass beside the airstrip
like a moth.

It would be blue and yellow, like the one in the photo on her uncle's wall. SCRATCH WITH THE CHICKENS OR FLY WITH THE EAGLES would be painted on the side. She would unsnap the cover and check the switch. Then she'd prime the engine and pull the silver propeller through.

She would climb into the cockpit. It would be cold inside; it would smell like fuel. She'd crack the throttle and turn on the switches. She'd push the button.

The engine would start, with a puff of blue smoke.

If she were a skywriter, she would bump along the grass beside the airstrip, using the rudder pedals to steer the plane. Then she'd stand on one brake to turn the nose into the wind.

She'd go through the checklist: controls, instruments, gas, trim—she'd check everything, just the way her uncle would have done it.

And everything would be okay.

She'd tighten her seat belt and pull her goggles down
over her eyes.

She'd let go of the brakes. She'd open the throttle. The plane
would rumble down the runway, gathering speed. She'd tap her
feet on the rudders to keep it going straight. She'd move the stick
forward. The trees would rush past faster and faster—and she
would feel that the plane was ready to leave the earth. So she
would pull the stick back, and the plane would lift into the air.

Below her, in a red-brick hospital, her uncle would be lying in a chrome bed with white sheets.

She'd fly low across the landscape. She'd buzz the roof of the hospital.

The nurse would part the curtains. Her uncle would open his eyes and look out the window.

She'd draw a heart, with white smoke. She'd roar back and
draw an arrow through it. She'd do a loop, then a hammerhead.
"Good-bye," she would write, in clouds.
Behind her, the letters would be blown across the sunset.

She'd land on a deserted highway on the coast and wait. Nobody would know she was there. Wind would gust in the grass. Waves would break on the shore.

Night would fall. Owls would hoot in the pines near the dunes, and crickets would sing.

And owls would hoot and crickets would sing outside her uncle's window. He would awaken—and know that the moon was on the horizon and beginning to rise.

She'd take off again.

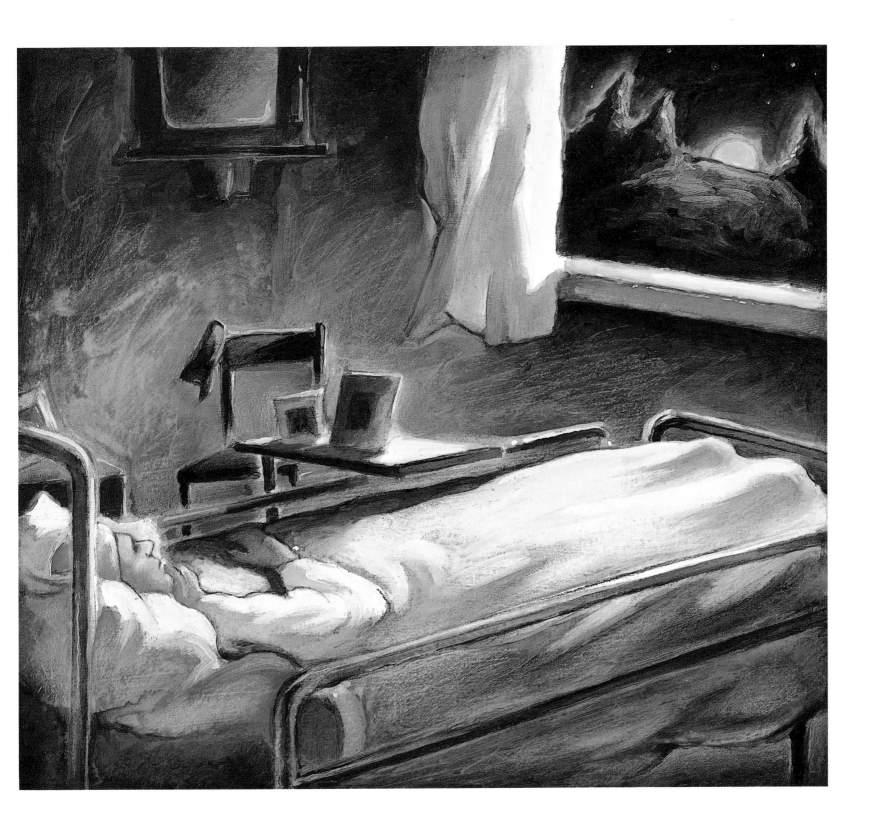

Airborne, in darkness, she'd climb out over the ocean,
following the black edge of the water. Below her, towns would
glimmer. Above her, stars would glimmer. Across the face of the
moon, she'd write—in silver letters:
    "I love you."
and then:
    "I'll see you in my dreams."

She was not a skywriter.

She was a little kid.

She would fly across the country on an airliner with a vapor trail behind it – a 767, like her uncle used to fly. She would stare out the window at the engine and the rivets on the wing.

The green position light would be steady on the wingtip. Below her, clouds would be stacked across the sky like dunes.

Hours would pass. The captain would announce the descent. She'd feel the power being pulled back – and the plane would sink into gray mist.

Her mother would try to prepare her:

"Don't forget, if you change your mind, you don't have to go to the hospital.

"Aunt Hannah says there's a woman in a cardigan sweater who walks the halls, asking over and over where she should sit – and there are two disabled men on the ward who look at the ceiling and only say 'A-a-a-h!' She says that it might frighten a child to see these men."

The plane would seem to sag and grow heavier, the closer it got to the ground.

"If you do go," her mother would tell her, "and decide not to go in and see him once we get there, that will be okay—it's difficult to say good-bye. Aunt Hannah and I will go in, and you can sit on a bench outside the room."

She would see signs and buildings, cars in the street—then empty fields and runway markers.

"In any event," her mother would say, "you must remember: He might not wake up. He might not even know you're there...."

The plane would land.
She would stand in the aisle with her mother behind her; the line of passengers would move slowly forward. On the way out,

she would look into the cockpit at the captain and the flight engineer, putting things into their kit bags, and the first officer — with three stripes on her uniform cuff and an eagle on her cap.

She would go to the hospital.

The "A-a-a-h!" men wouldn't frighten her; she might even say hello to them, might ask the nurse their names. If the woman in the cardigan sweater asked her where she should sit, she would suggest that she sit on a bench with her aunt and her mother.

Then she would walk alone into the room where her uncle
was sleeping.

His breathing would be unsteady; his chest would rise and fall.
She'd look at his face. It would be the same, but different.
She'd stand by the side of his bed and hold his hand.

He might not know that she was standing there.
But she would know that she was standing there. And she
would know what she would say to him.

And she would know what she would write to him — if she were a skywriter.

DATE DUE

APR 1 2 1995	
APR 1 2 1995	
JUL 1 2 1995	
NOV 2 1 1995	DEC 1 8 1999
FEB 2 3 1999	
DEC 1 8 1999	MAR 07 2000
	OCT 0 0 2000
	MAY 2 3 2001
NOV 4 2001	
NOV 2 0 2001	
APR 3 0 2002	

Demco, Inc. 38-293